Sitting In My BOX

Marshall Cavendish Corporation, 99 White Plains Road, Tarrytown, NY 10591
www.marshallcavendish.us/kids

Marshall Cavendish *Classics*

Marshall Cavendish is bringing classic titles from children's literature
back into print for a new generation.
We have selected titles that have withstood the test of time,
and we welcome any suggestions for future titles in this program.
To learn more, visit our Web site: **www.marshallcavendish.us/kids.**

Library of Congress Cataloging-in-Publication Data

Lillegard, Dee.
  Sitting in my box / by Dee Lillegard ; illustrated by Jon Agee. — 1st
Marshall Cavendish Classics ed.
    p. cm.
  Summary: The box in which all the animals are sitting gets more
and more crowded until a hungry flea comes along.
  ISBN 978-0-7614-5646-9
  [1. Boxes–Fiction. 2. Animals–Fiction.] I. Agee, Jon, ill. II. Title.
PZ7.L6275Si 2010
  [E]–dc22   2009007936

Printed in China (E)
First Marshall Cavendish Classics edition, 2009
3 5 6 4 2

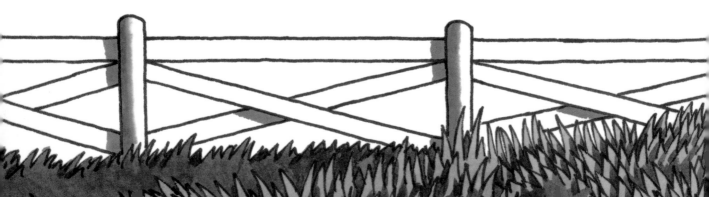

For Brett,
who remembers sitting in his box
—D.L.

Marshall Cavendish Childre

Sitting In My BOX

by **Dee Lillegard**

pictures by **Jon Agee**

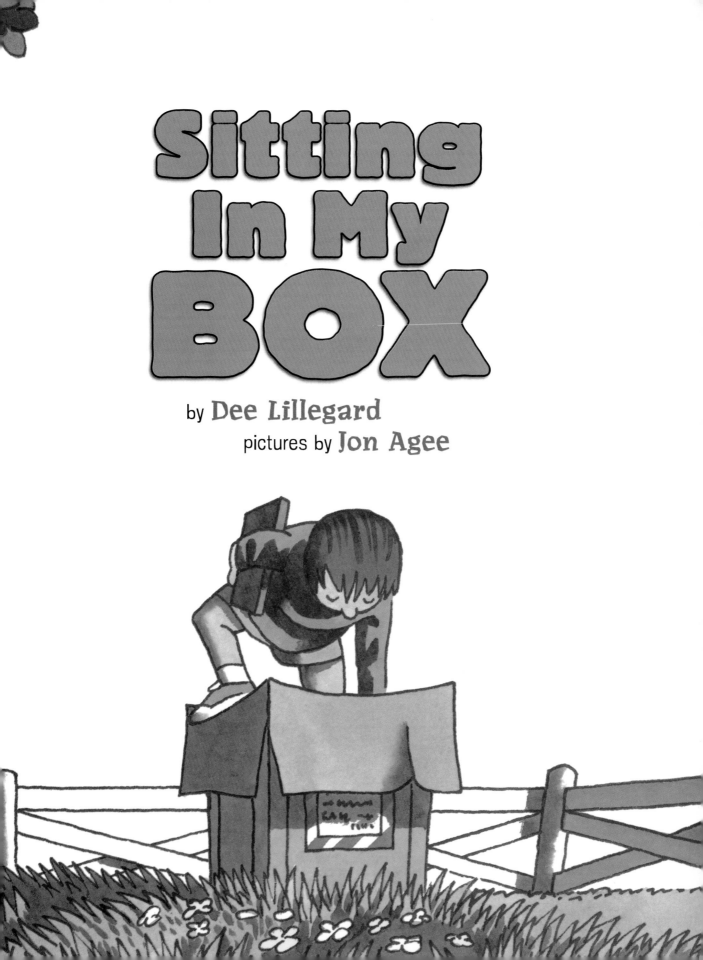

Sitting in my box.

A tall giraffe knocks.

"Let me, let me in."
So I move over.

Sitting in my box.
An old gray
elephant knocks.

"Let me, let me in."
So we both
move over.

Sitting in my box.
A big baboon knocks.

"Let me, let me in."
So we all move over.

Sitting in my box.
A grumpy lion knocks.

"Let me, let me in."
So we all move over.

Sitting in my box.
A hippopotamus knocks.

"Let me, let me in."
So we *all* move over.

Standing in my box.
There's no room to sit.

"Wait a minute!
This box has
too much in it."

Sitting in my box.
Along comes a flea.
A flea *never* knocks.
He jumps right in.

He bites the hippo
and the grumpy lion.

He bites the baboon
and the old gray
elephant.

He bites the tall giraffe.

That's why I'm sitting in my box...

just me.